SWASTIK BHARAT

UNKNOWN MANOJ

SWASTIK BHARAT

Moral of this book

This book is about to spread Education to all over United India Citizen.

Swastik Bharat also form Political Party, to support Nationalist leader and Party of our country and first five years Supporter and Followers will do publicity in our people and make our supporter educationally strong.

Nobody has written this book I am only medium to write this holy book which I am heard in my dream.

This book will translate and publish in all United Indian Language and World Language.

UNITED INDIA REGION PEOPLE

Hindu region people are very brave but we have forgotten to read Vedas, holy book and Puranas so from 1000 years enemy is attacking us. If we start reading Vedas, Puranas, holy book etc. our mind becomes very strong and we gain so much knowledge that we can defeat anybody. Nobody in world brave than us in fighting war as we have defeated Asur who are most powerful in Earth.only name of God ,Vedas are mention in this holy book for details they should learn Vedas,Puranas,Ramayana,Mahabharata etc.

BHARAT MATA

Bharat Mata (Mother India) is a national Symbol of India (Bharat) as a mother goddess. In the visual arts she is commonly seen in a red or saffron-coloured sari and holding a national flag; she sometimes stands on a lotus and is accompanied by a lion.

Our mother and motherland is to be considered higher than heaven in our old Sanskrit literature, the idea of the mother goddess, Bharat Mata, comes in people mind from birth. She appeared first in the popular Bengali language-novel Anandmath in a form inseparable from the Hindu goddesses Durga and Kali.

Temple/Mandir

Now world has change it is not Vedic period Temple want reform.

Temple or Mandir is a Place where God and Goddess live in the form of sculpture/ murti and Hindu pray and worship there. Every Hindu duty is to come and worship in Mandir and protects the Mandir from enemy (who do not come to worship in temple or who hate our Religion and Hindu dharma). Any Hindu people, who live in united India region and believer of hindutva, can come to worship in Mandir. No any rule to not allow to any Hindu caste and class as it has not written in our any holy book it is rumours to divide Hindu and hindutva believer.

Principle Rule of Temple

1. In every District one main temple and all temple of that district shall be guide by main temple.
2. One temple protector, sixteen supporter of temple protector and each supporter have sixteen hundred worship followers (Man, woman, children, sanyasi, sadhu etc.) And every followers and supporter has to follow the advice of Temple protector and his decision or advice is final.
3. Temple protector terms are for one year's only and after that he will be temple follower only no second terms is allowed in any case.
4. Temple protector shall be wise and educated man or woman and we have to provide respect in society.
5. All four dham (char dham) and other our holy religious city has sixteen thousands of strong followers and they shall be ready to any time to protect temple.
6. Temple protector, temple supporter and temple follower should be brave, and knowledge of war fighting policy and for this personal combat fighting training should be given from childhood with Education to both male and female.
7. Temple protector should always ready to help another district temple protector

for any help to temple in any action.

8. All char dham and our holy city up to 16miles around should be clean and properly managed and no another worship places who hate Hindu god and temple and who have no believe on murti puja or unauthorised construction should be available there it should be move to another location in 25 years period and become aggressive always for destruction.
9. Respect of woman, truth and justice is Temple main rule. Women & girl should be trained to become brave, good character, self-dependent and in combat fighting.
10. No any caste system shall be followed in temple.
11. Temple should make policy and advisory rule to run the temple administration and it is common to all over united India district temple, take help from Government administration in policy making.
12. Temple Protector only good for Hindu religion.
13. Temple protector should help to make temple follower self-dependent and provide job and work to everyone with support of Government.
14. Temple need sacrifice and hard work every Hindu people ready for it.
15. Temple should support to Government, Constitution, administration and other Government agency and follow the rule and in any situation temple should help Defence and army in first priority with full support with everything and provide any time his follower to war to support army.
16. Temple should teach his student and followers to become aggressive and take our land one by one may be it will take 50-100 years but aggressive to take our land will never stop.
17. Temple should support his follower in Education and administrative job. World class education should be providing to our children.
18. In every village of Temple each district 10% land should be of Gram sabha for Temple, Animals, Jungle etc. and it shall be never taken by anybody and if anybody has captured make them free officially or patta to anybody till earth alive.
19. Temple should accept sacrifice to die but never accept separation of country. Temple should teach his follower only to Unite Indian region again. Punish them who talk about separation of country in the name of Language, culture, etc.A

weak people,enemy people,incapable people,jealous people and otherlike this people always for their personal profit they start to divide people in the name of language,culture,caste etc. and start demending for seperation,temple should stop this type of people and punish them so that no body raise the voice of seperation.

20. All united Indian region district Temple should be in one chain with coordination if any temple required help anywhere support of follower should reach in time.
21. Temple protector and supporter should do work silently and do not involved in public dealing as they are respected person.
22. Temple protector head terms are for only one year. Temple protector head should be from every caste one by one residing in that district. Vedas should be read by all people so that they know that there is no any caste system it is for everyone and they can describe to their people who do not read Vedas and holy book.
23. Temple should take minimum donation from shopkeepers and businessman doing business in temple area for to expense in temple and balance should be paid to Temple protector and temple protector supporter and one by one to all follower of temple.
24. Temple protector and Temple protector sixteen supporters should be paid monthly good salary.
25. Temple should not give any money to beggar as it should be beggar free but give money and take work from them and temple area should be clean.
26. Temple should look after the age of sixty years to all people of the district and pay money monthly or provide them to survive good life as after sixty years they are god and temple people but who are getting pension or any funds from government or private do not give any monthly payment to them.
27. After every fifty years rule should reform as per their time but any good rule for temple it should reform any time.
28. Who have Hindu name he is considered as Hindu. If any Hindu boy or girl marriage to another religion he or she have to convert in Hinduism They cannot convert to another religion. Conversion should be done who have by any reason or situation and convert them to in Hinduism.
29. Temple should give respect to another country religion which is beyond the

United India region and make good relation and friendship with that country and always welcome them. Make all worlds your friends.

30. Always respect the minority whose God, Guru, Panth, etc. is from united Indian region because they all are our people and some difference required.
31. Temple follow vedas,puranas and other holy book and real history only.God has send Arya people directly in indian region when Earth formed and all indians including asur are also arya,
32. Temple should teach people about truth and justice and to follow it.Temple should mainly focussed on Education of people and teach people not to believe in any superstition and hypocrite.

VED

The Ved are a large body of religious texts originating in ancient India. Composed in Vedic Sanskrit, the texts constitute the oldest layer of Sanskrit literature and the oldest scriptures of Hindu.

There are four type of Ved the Rigved, the Yajurved, the Samved and the Atharvaved. Each Veda has four subdivisions – the Samhita mantra and benedictions), the Aranyaka (book on rituals, ceremonies, sacrifices and symbolic-sacrifices), the Brahmana (An expression of opinions on rituals, ceremonies and sacrifices), and the Upanishads (pages discussing meditation, philosophy and spiritual knowledge). Some scholars add a fifth category – the Upasanas (worship).

Ved are sruti ("what is heard"), to recognize or difference them from other religious texts, which are called smriti ("what is remembered"). Hindu consider the Ved to be apaurusey, which means "not of a man, superhuman" and "impersonal, authorless," revelations of sacred sounds and texts heard by ancient sages after intense meditation.

The Ved have been orally transmitted with the help of elaborate mnemonic techniques. The mantras, the oldest part of the Ved, are recited in the modern age for their phonology rather than the semantics, and are considered to be "primordial rhythms of creation", preceding the forms to which they refer. By reciting them the Universe is regenerated, "by enlivening and nourishing the forms of creation at their base."

Four Ved

The canonical division of the Ved is fourfold (turīya)

1. Rigved
2. Yajurved
3. Samaved
4. Atharvaved

Of these, the first three were the principal original division, also called "trayi vidya"; that is, "the triple science" of reciting hymns (Rigved), performing sacrifices (Yajurved), and chanting songs (Samaved). Only one version of the Rigveda is known to have survived into the modern era. Several different versions of the Samaveda and the Atharvaved are known, and many different versions of the Yajurved have been found in different parts of Asia region.

Rigved

The Rigveda Samhita is the oldest extant Hindu text. It is a collection of 1,028 Vedic Sanskrit hymns and 10,600 verses in all, organized into ten books (Sanskrit: mandalas). The hymns are dedicated to Rigved deities.

The Rigved is structured based on clear principles. The Ved begins with a small book addressed to Agni, Indra, Soma and other gods, all arranged according to decreasing total number of hymns in each deity collection, for each deity series, the hymns progress from longer to shorter ones, but the number of hymns per book increases. Finally, the meter too is systematically arranged from jagati and tristubh to anustubh and gayatri as the text progresses.

Samaved

The samved Samhit consists of 1549 stanzas, taken almost entirely (except for 75 mantras) from the Rigved. While its earliest parts are believed to date from as early as the Rigvedic period, the existing compilation dates from the post-Rigvedic Mantra period of Vedic Sanskrit, between 1200 and 1000 BCE or "slightly later," roughly contemporary with the Atharvaved and the Yajurved.

The Samaved samhita has two major parts. The first part includes four melody collections (gana) and the second part three verse "books" (arcika). A melody in the song books corresponds to a verse in the arcika books. Just as in the Rigved, the early sections of Samaved typically begin with hymns to Agni and Indra but shift to the abstract. Their meters shift also in a descending order. The songs in the later sections of the Samaved have the least deviation from the hymns derived from the Rigved.

Yajurved

The Yajur Samhita consists of prose mantras. It is a compilation of ritual offering formulas that were said by a priest while an individual performed ritual actions such as those before the Yajna fire. The core text of the Yajurveda falls within the classical Mantra period of Vedic Sanskrit at the end of the 2nd millennium BCE - younger than the Rigveda, and roughly contemporary with the Atharvaveda the Rigvedic Khilani, and the Samaved.

The earliest and most ancient layer of Yajurved samhita includes about 1,875 verses that are distinct yet borrow and build upon the foundation of verses in Rigveda. Unlike the Samaveda which is almost entirely based on Rigved mantras and structured as songs, the Yajurved samhitas are in prose, and they are different from earlier Vedic texts linguistically. The Yajur Ved has been the primary source of information about sacrifices during Vedic times and associated rituals.

Atharvaved

The Artharvaved samhita is the text belonging to the Atharvan and Angirasa poets. It has about 760 hymns, and about 160 of the hymns are in common with the Rigved. Most of the verses are metrical, but some sections are in prose. Two different versions of the text – the Paippalāda and the Śaunakīya – have survived into the modern times The Atharvaved was not considered as a Ved in the Vedic era, and was accepted as a Veda in late 1st millennium BCE. It was compiled last, probably around 900 BCE, although some of its material may go back to the time of the Rigveda, or earlier.

The Atharvaved is sometimes called the "Veda of magical formulas", an epithet declared to be incorrect by other scholars. The Samhita layer of the text likely represents a developing 2nd millennium BCE tradition of magico-religious rites to address superstitious anxiety, spells to remove maladies believed to be caused by demons, and herbs- and nature-derived potions as medicine.

The Atharvaved has been a primary source for information about Vedic culture, the customs and beliefs, the aspirations and frustrations of everyday Vedic life, as well as those associated with kings and governance. The text also includes hymns dealing with the two major rituals of passage – marriage and cremation. The Atharvveda also dedicates significant portion of the text asking the meaning of a ritual.

PURAN

Puran is a vast genre of Indian literature about a wide range of topics, particularly about legends and other traditional lore. The Puran are known for the intricate layers of symbolism depicted within their stories. Composed originally in Sanakrit but in other Indian languages, several of these texts are named after major Hindu deities such as Vishnu, Shiva, Brahma and Shakti. The Puranic genre of literature is found in Hinduism .

The Puranic literature is encyclopaedic, and it includes diverse topics such as cosmogony, cosmology, genealogies of gods, goddesses, kings, heroes, sages, and demigods, folk tales, pilgrimages, temples, medicine, astronomy, grammar, mineralogy, humor, love stories, as well as theology and philosophy. The content is highly inconsistent across the Puran, and each Puran has survived in numerous manuscripts which are themselves inconsistent. The Hindu Maha Puran are traditionally attributed to "Vyasa".

There are 18 Mukhya Puran (Major Puran) and 18 Upa Puran (Minor Puran), with over 400,000 verses. The first versions of various Puran were likely to have been composed between 3rd and 10th century CE. The Puran do not enjoy the authority of a scripture in sanathan, but are considered as Smritis.

They have been influential in the Hindu culture, inspiring major national and regional annual festivals of Hinduism. Their role and value as sectarian religious texts and historical texts has been controversial because all Puran praise many gods and goddesses and "their sectarianism is far less clear cut" than assumed, states Ludo Rocher. The religious practices included in them are considered Vaidika (congruent with Vedic literature), because they do not preach initiation into Tantra. The Bhadavata Puran has been among the most celebrated and popular text in the Puranic genre, and is, in the opinion of some, of non-dualistic tenor.

Lord Ram

Ram as Ramachandra is a major deity in Sanathan. He is the seventh and one of the most popular avatars of Vishnu. In Ram-centric traditions of Hinduism, he is considered the Supreme Being.

Ram is said to have been born to Kaushalya and Dasharath in Ayodhya, the ruler of the Kingdom of Kosla. His siblings included Lakshman, Bharat and Shatrughn. He married Sita. Though born in a royal family, their life is described in the Hindu texts as one challenged by unexpected changes such as an exile into impoverished and difficult circumstances, ethical questions and moral dilemmas. Of all their travails, the most notable is the kidnapping of Sita by demon-king Ravan, followed by the determined and epic efforts of Rama and Lakshmana to gain her freedom and destroy the evil Ravan against great odds. The entire life story of Ram, Sita and their companions allegorically discusses duties, rights and social responsibilities of an individual. It illustrates dharma and dharmic living through model characters.

Ram is especially important to Vaishnavism. He is the central figure of the ancient Hindu epic Ramayana, a text historically popular in the South Asian and Southeast Asian cultures. His ancient legends have attracted bhasya (commentaries) and extensive secondary literature and inspired performance arts. Two such texts, for example, are the Adhyatma Ramayana – a spiritual and theological treatise considered foundational by Ramanandi monasteries, and the Ramcharitmanas – a popular treatise that inspires thousands of Ram Lila festival performances during autumn every year in India. Ayodhya is the birth palace of Ram and huge universe Temple is there named Ram temple. Another temple is plan to construct in Arunachal Pradesh,Tripura,Manipur,Meghalaya and murti srructure should be of stone and big.

"Jai Shree Ram" is our War Slogan and we will win all our war with Demon People.

LORD KRISHNA

Krishna is a major Deity in Sanathan. He is worshipped as the eighth avatar of Vishnu and also as the supreme God in his own right. He is the god of protection, compassion, tenderness, and love; and is one of the most popular and widely revered among Indian divinities. Krishna's birthday is celebrated every year by Hindus on Krishna Janmashtami according to the linisolar Hindu calendar, which falls in late August or early September.

The anecdotes and narratives of Krishna's life are generally titled as Krishna Lela. He is a central character in the Mahabharata, the Bhagavata Puran, the Brahna Vaivarta Purana and the Bhagavad Gita, and is mentioned in many Hindu philosophical, theological and mythological texts. They portray him in various perspectives: a god-child, a prankster, a model lover, a divine hero, and as the universal Supreme Being. His iconography reflects these legends, and shows him in different stages of his life, such as an infant eating butter, a young boy playing a flute, a young boy with Radha or surrounded by women devotees, or a friendly charioteer giving counsel to Arjuna. The name and synonyms of Krishna have been traced to 1st millennium BCE literature and cults. In some sub-traditions, Krishna is worshipped as Svayam Bhagavan (the Supreme God) and it sometimes known as Krishnaism. These sub-traditions arose in the context of the medieval era Bhakti movement. Krishna-related literature has inspired numerous performance arts such as Bharatanatyam, Kathakali, Kuchipudi, Odissi and Manipuri dance. He is a pan-Hindu god, but is particularly revered in some locations such as Vrindavan in Uttar Pradesh,Dwarka and Junagadh in Gujarat ,the Jagannatha aspect in Odisha,Mayapur in West Bengal in the form of Vithoba in Pandharpur ,Maharashtra , Shrinathji at Nathdwara in Rajasthan , Udipi Krishna in Karnataka ,Parthasarathy in Tamil Nadu, Partasarathy in Aranmula, Kerla and Guruvayooraooan in Guruvayoor in Kerala. Since the 1960s, the worship of Krishna has also spread to the Western world and to Africa, largely due to the work of the International society for Krishna Consciousness (ISKCON).

Goddess Sita

Sita is a Hindu goddess and the female protagonist of the Hindu epic, Ramayan. She is the consort of Ram, the avatar of the god Vishnu and is regarded as a form of Vishnu's wife Lakshmi. She is also the chief goddess of Rama-centric Hindu traditions. Sita is known for her dedication, self-sacrifice, courage, and purity. She is one of the seventeen national heroes of Nepal.

Described as the daughter of Bhumi (the earth), Sita is brought up as the adopted daughter of King Janak of Videha. Sita, in her youth, chooses Ram, the prince of Ayodhya as her husband in a swayamvara. After the swayamvar, she accompanies her husband to his kingdom, but later chooses to accompany her husband, along with her brother-in-law Lakshman, in his exile. While in exile, the trio settles in the Dandak forest from where she is abducted by Ravana, the Rakshas king of Lanka. She is imprisoned in the garden of Ashok Vatika, in Lanka, until she is rescued by Ram, who slays her captor. After the war, in some versions of the epic, Ram asks Sita to undergo Agni Pariksha (an or deal of fire), by which she proves her purity, before she is accepted by Ram, which for the first time makes his brother Lakshman get angry at him.

In some versions of the epic, Maya Sita, an illusion created by Agni, takes Sita's place and is abducted by Ravan and suffers his captivity, while the real Sita hides in the fire. Some scriptures also mention her previous birth being Vedavati, a woman Ravan tries to molest. After proving her purity, Rama and Sita return to Ayodhya, where they are crowned as king and queen. One day, man questions Sita's purity and in order to prove her innocence and maintain his own and the kingdom's dignity, Ram sends Sita into the forest near the sage Valmiki's ashram. Years later, Sita returns to the womb of her mother, the Earth, for release from a cruel world and as a testimony of her purity, after she reunites her two sons Kush and Lav with their father Ram.

LORD BRAHMA

Brahma is a Hindu God, referred to as "The Creator" within the Trimurti, the trinity of supreme divinity that includes Vishnu, and Shiva. He is associated with creation, knowledge, and the Vedas. Brahma is prominently mentioned in Hindu cosmogony.

In some Puranas, he created himself in a golden embryo known as the Hiranyagarbha.

.Brahma is frequently identified with the Vedic god Prajapati During the post-Vedic period, Brahma was a prominent deity and his sect existed; however, by the 7th century, he had lost his significance. He was also overshadowed by other major deities like Vishnu, Shiva and Devi and demoted to the role of a secondary creator, who was created by the major deities. Along with other such Hindu deities, Brahma is sometimes viewed as a form (saguna) of the otherwise formless (nirguna) Brahman, the ultimate metaphysical reality in Vedantic Hinduism.

Brahma is commonly depicted as a red or golden complexioned bearded man, with four heads and hands. His four heads represent the four Ved and are pointed to the four cardinal directions. He is seated on a lotus and hisvahana (mount) is a hamsa (swan). According to the scriptures, Brahma created his children from his mind and thus, they are referred to as Manasputra.

In contemporary Hinduism, Brahma does not enjoy popular worship and has substantially less importance than the other two members of the Trimurti. Brahma is revered in the ancient texts, yet rarely worshiped as a primary deity in India, owing to the absence of any significant sect dedicated to his veneration, which also impacts his consort Saraswati. Very few temples dedicated to him exist in India, the most famous being the Brahma Temple, Pushkar in Rajasthan. Some Brahma temples are found outside India, such as at the Erawan shrine in Bangkok.

LORD VISHNU

Vishnu also known as Narayan and Hari is one of the principal deities of Hinduism. He is the Supreme Being within Vaishnavism, one of the major traditions within contemporary Hinduism.

Vishnu is known as "The Preserver" within the Trimurti, the triple deity of supreme divinity that includes Brahma and Shiva. In Vaishnavism tradition, Vishnu is the Supreme Being who creates, protects and transforms the universe. In the Shaktism tradition, the Goddess, or Devi, is described as one of the supreme, yet Vishnu is revered along with Shiva and Brahma. A goddess is stated to be the energy and creative power (Shakti) of each, with Lakshmi the equal complementary partner of Vishnu. He is one of the five equivalent deities in Panchayatana puja of the Smart tradition of Hinduism.

According to the Vaishnavism sect, the highest form of Ishvar is with qualities (Saguna), and has certain form but is limitless, transcendent and unchanging absolute Brahman, and the primal Atman (Self) of the universe. There are many both benevolent and fearsome depictions of Vishnu. In benevolent aspects, he is depicted as an omniscient sleeping on the coils of the serpent Adishesha (who represents time) floating in the primeval ocean of milk called Kshira Sagara with consort Lakshmi.

Whenever the world is threatened with evil, chaos, and destructive forces, Vishnu descends in the form of an avatar (incarnation) to restore the cosmic order and protect Dharma. Dashavatara are the ten primary avatars (incarnations) of Vishnu. Out of the ten, Rama and Krishna avatars are most important.

LORD SHANKAR

Lord shankar or Shiva, also known as Mahadeva ('The Great God'), is one of the principal deities of Hinduism. God Shiva is said to be the controller of time itself and has the responsibility of carrying out the process of destruction at the end of creation. In Sanskrit language, Kala means time. He is also called Mahakala as all the three times—past, present and future—lie within him and are from him. He is the Supreme Being in Shaivism, one of the major traditions within Hinduism.

Shiva has pre-Vedic roots, and the figure of Shiva as we know him today is an amalgamation of various older non-Vedic and Vedic deities, including the Rig Vedic storm god Rudra who may also have non-Vedic origins, into a single major deity.

Shiva is known as "The Destroyer" within the Trimurti, the triple deity of supreme divinity that also includes Brahma and Vishnu. In the Shaivite tradition, Shiva is the Supreme Lord who creates, protects and transforms the universe. In the Shakta tradition, the Goddess, or Devi, is described as one of the supreme, yet Shiva is revered along with Vishnu and Brahma. A goddess is stated to be the energy and creative power (Shakti) of each, with Parvati (sati) the equal complementary partner of Shiva. He is one of the five equivalent deities in Panchayatana puja of the Smarta tradition of Hinduism.

Shiva is the primal Atman (Self) of the universe. There are many both benevolent and fearsome depictions of Shiva. In benevolent aspects, he is depicted as an omniscient Yogi who lives an ascetic life on Mount Kailash as well as a householder with his wife Parvati and his two children, Ganesha and Kartikeya. In his fierce aspects, he is often depicted slaying demons. Shiva is also known as Adiyogi Shiva, regarded as the patron god of yoga, meditation and the arts.

The iconographical attributes of Shiva are the serpent around his neck, the adorning crescent moon, the holy river Ganga flowing from his matted hair, the third eye on his forehead (the eye that turns everything in front of it into ashes when opened), the trishula or trident as his weapon, and the damaru drum. He is usually worshipped in the aniconic form of lingam.

Shiva is a pan-Hindu deity, revered widely by Hindus in United India, Nepal, Sri Lanka and Indonesia (especially in Java and Bali).

GODDESS PARVATI

Parvati or Gauri is the Hindu goddess of power, nourishment, harmony, devotion, and motherhood. She is considered to be Devi in her complete form. She is the principal goddess of Shaivism. She is also one of the central deities of the goddess-oriented sect called Shaktism. Along with Lakshmi and Saraswati, she forms the Tridev.

Parvati is the wife of the Hindu god Shiva. She is the reincarnation of Sati, the first wife of Shiva who immolated herself during a Vaina (fire-sacrifice). Parvati is the daughter of the mountain king Himayan and queen Mena. Parvati is the mother of Hindu deities Ganesha and Kartikeya. The Puranas also referenced her to be the sister of the river goddess Ganga and the preserver god Vishnu. For Shaivites, she is considered to be the divine energy between a man and a woman, like the energy of Shiva and Shakti. For Vaishnavites, she is respected as Vishnu Vilasini, or "she who dwells on Vishnu", as stated in the Mahishasura Mardini Stotram.

Parvati is generally portrayed as a gentle, nurturing mother goddess, but is also associated with several terrible forms to vanquish evil and demons such as Durga, Kali, the ten mahavidyas and Navadurga.

Parvati is an embodiment of Shakti. In Shaivism, she is the recreative energy and power of Shiva, and she is the cause of a bond that connects all beings and a means of their spiritual release. She is also well known as Kamarupa (one who give a shape to your desire) and Kameshwari (one who fulfil your all desires). In Hindu temples dedicated to her and Shiva, she is symbolically represented as the argha. She is found extensively in ancient Indian literature, and her statues and iconography grace Hindu temples all over South Asia and Southeast Asia.

GODDESS LAKSHMI

Lakshmi ('she who leads to one's goal') also known as Shri is one of the principal goddesses in Hinduism. She is the goddess of wealth, fortune, power, beauty, fertility and prosperity, and associated with Maya ("Illusion"). Along with Parvati and Saraswati, she forms the Tridev of Hindu goddesses.

Within the Goddess-oriented Shaktism, Lakshmi is venerated as the prosperity aspect of the Mother goddess. Lakshmi is both the consort and the divine energy (Shakti) of the Hindu god Vishnu, the Supreme Being of Vaishnavism; she is also the Supreme Goddess in the sect and assists Vishnu to create, protect and transform the universe. She is an especially prominent figure in Sri Vaishnavism, in which devotion to Lakshmi is deemed to be crucial to reach Vishnu. Whenever Vishnu descended on the earth as an avatar, Lakshmi accompanied him as consort, as Sita and Radha or Rukmini as consorts of Vishnu's avatars Ram and Krishn, respectively. The eight prominent manifestations of Lakshmi, the Ashtalakshmi symbolize the eight sources of wealth.

Lakshmi is depicted in Indian art as an elegantly dressed, prosperity-showering golden-coloured woman standing or sitting in padmasana on a lotus throne, while holding a lotus in her hand, symbolising fortune, self-knowledge, and spiritual liberation. Her iconography shows her with four hands, which represent the four aspects of human life important to Hindu culture: dharma, Kama, artha, and moksha. Lakshmi Sahasranama of Skanda Purana, Lakshmi Tantra, Markandeya Purana, Devi Mahatmya and Vedic scriptures describes Lakshmi as having eight or eighteen hands and as sitting on Garud, Lion or Tiger.

Archaeological discoveries and ancient coins suggest the recognition and reverence for Lakshmi existing by the 1st millennium BCE. Lakshmi's iconography and statues have also been found in Hindu temples throughout Southeast Asia, estimated to be from the second half of the 1st millennium CE. The day of Lakshmi Puja during Navarati, and the festivals of Deepavali and Sharad Purnima (Kojagiri Purnima) are celebrated in her honour.

GODDESS SARASWATI

Saraswati is the Hindu goddess of knowledge, music, art, speech, wisdom, and learning. She is one of the Tridev, along with the goddesses Lakshmi and Parvati

The earliest known mention of Saraswati as a goddess is in the Rigved She has remained significant as a goddess from the Vedic period through the modern period of Hindu traditions. She is generally shown to have four arms, holding a book, a rosary, a water pot, and a musical instrument called the veena. Each of these items has a symbolic meaning in Hinduism.

Some Hindus celebrate the festival of Vasant Panchami (the fifth day of spring, and also known as Saraswati Puja and Saraswati Jayanti in many regions of India) in her honour, and mark the day by helping young children learn how to write the letters of the alphabet on that day.

The goddess Saraswati is often depicted as a beautiful woman dressed in pure white often seated on a white lotus, which symbolizes light, knowledge and truth. She not only embodies knowledge but also the experience of the highest reality. Her iconography is typically in white themes from dress to flowers to swan – the colour symbolizing Sattwa Guna or purity, discrimination for true knowledge, insight and wisdom.

Her dhyana mantra describes her to be as white as the moon, clad in a white dress, bedecked in white ornaments, radiating with beauty, holding a book and a pen in her hands (the book represents knowledge)

She is generally shown to have four arms, but sometimes just two. When shown with four hands, those hands symbolically mirror her husband Brahma's four heads, representing manas (mind, sense), buddhi (intellect, reasoning), citta (imagination, creativity), and ahamkara (self-consciousness, ego). Brahma represents the abstract, while she represents action and reality.

The four hands hold items with symbolic meaning – a pustaka (book or script), a mala (rosary, garland), a water pot and a musical instrument (veena). The book she holds symbolizes the Vedas representing the universal, divine, eternal, and true knowledge as well as all forms of learning. A mala of crystals, representing the power of meditation, inner reflection, and spirituality. A pot of water represents the purifying power to separate right from wrong, the clean from the unclean, and essence from the inessential. In some texts, the pot of water is symbolism for soma – the drink that liberates and leads to knowledge. The most famous feature on Saraswati is a musical instrument called a veena, represents all creative arts and sciences, and her holding it symbolizes expressing knowledge that creates harmony. Saraswati is also associated with anuraga, the love for and rhythm of music, which represents all emotions and feelings expressed in speech or music.

A hamsa – either a swan or a goose – is often shown near her feet. In Sanathan mythology, the hamsa is a sacred bird, which if offered a mixture of milk and water, is said to be able to drink the milk alone. It thus symbolizes the ability to discriminate between good and evil, essence from the outward show, and the eternal from the evanescent. Due to her association with the swan, Saraswati is also referred to as Hamsavahini, which means "she who has a hamsa as her vehicle". The swan is also a symbolism for spiritual perfection, transcendence and moksha.

Sometimes a citramekhala (also called mayura, peacock) is shown beside the goddess. The peacock symbolizes colourful splendour, the celebration of dance, and – as the devourer of snakes – the alchemical ability to transmute the serpent poison of self into the radiant plumage of enlightenment.

She is usually depicted near a flowing river or another body of water, which depiction may constitute a reference to her early history as a river goddess.

She is a part of the Tridevi, the triad of great Goddesses. She represents the Sattwa Guna, and Jnana Shakti.

GODDESS DURGA

Durga is a major deity in Hinduism. She is worshipped as a one of principal aspects of the mother goddess Mahadevi and is one of the most popular and widely revered among Indian divinities. She is associated with protection, strength, motherhood, destruction and wars. According to Devi-Bhagavata Purana she is one of five forms of Goddess Bhuvaneshvari. Her legend centres around combating evils and demonic forces that threaten peace, prosperity, and Dharma the power of good over evil. Durga is believed to unleash her divine wrath against the wicked for the liberation of the oppressed, and entails destruction to empower creation. Historians of religion and art tend to trace the earliest depiction of Durga to the seals of Indus Valley Civilization. However, this claim lacks direct visual evidence from the site. There are several hints to her in the early Vedic texts and by the time of the epics, she emerges as an independent deity. Durga is seen as a motherly figure and often depicted as a beautiful woman, riding a lion or tiger, with many arms each carrying a weapon and often defeating demons she is widely worshipped by the followers of the goddess centric sect, Shaktism, and has importance in other denominations like Shaivism and Vaishnavism. Under these traditions, Durga is associated and identified with other deities. There are many devotees of Goddess Durga who recite Saptashloki Durga Saptashati to seek her blessings.

The two most important texts of Shaktism, Devi Mahatmya and Devi-Bhagavat reveres Devi or Shakti (goddess) as the primordial creator of the universe and the Brahman (ultimate truth and reality). While all major texts of Hinduism mention and revere the goddess, these two texts center around her as the primary divinity.

Durga has a significant following all over United India, and Nepal, particularly in its Indian states such as Bengal, Odisha, Jharkhand, Assam, Arunachal Pradesh, Nagaland, Manipur, Meghalaya, Tripura, Sikkim , Bihar, Gujarat, Maharashtra, Tamil Nadu, Kerala, Andhra Pradesh,Karnataka,Rajashthan,Pondichary,Jammu,Kashmir,Laddakh,Punjab,Himachal Pradesh, Uttar Pradesh, Uttarakhand,Sindh,Madhya Pradesh, Chhattisgarh etc. and all over Union territory of United India. Durga is revered after spring and autumn harvests, especially during the festivals of Durga Puja and Navratri.

GODDESS KALI

Kali, also known as Dakshina Kalika, is a Hindu goddess who is considered to be the master of death, time and change. She is also said to be the Parvati, the supreme of all powers, or the ultimate reality.

Kali's earliest appearance is when she emerged from Lord Shiv. She is the ultimate manifestation of Shakti and the mother of all living beings. She destroys the evil in order to protect the innocent. Over time, Kali has been worshipped by devotional movements and tantric sects variously as the Divine Mother, Mother of the Universe, Adi Shakti, or Parvati Shakta Hindu and Tantric sects additionally worship her as the ultimate reality or Brahman. She is also seen as the divine protector and the one who bestows moksha or liberation.

In Kali's most famous legend, Durga and her assistants, the Matrikas, wound the demon Raktabij, in various ways and with a variety of weapons in an attempt to destroy him. They soon find that they have worsened the situation for with every drop of blood that is dripped from Raktabij, he reproduces a duplicate of himself. The battlefield becomes increasingly filled with his duplicates; Durga summons Kali to combat the demons. The Devi Mahatmyam describes.

Out of the surface of her (Durga's) forehead, fierce with frown, issued suddenly Kali of terrible countenance, armed with a sword and noose. Bearing the strange Khatvanga (skull-topped staff), decorated with a garland of skulls, clad in a tiger's skin, very appalling owing to her emaciated flesh, with gaping mouth, fearful with her tongue lolling out, having deep reddish eyes, filling the regions of the sky with her roars, falling upon impetuously and slaughtering the great asuras in that army, she devoured those hordes of the foes of the devas.

Kali consumes Raktabij and his duplicates, and dances on the corpses of the slain. In Devi Mahatmya version of this story, Kali is also described as a Matrika and as a Shakti or power of Devi. She is given the epithet Camuṇḍa (Chamunda), i.e. the slayer of the demons Chanda and Munda. Chamunda is very often identified with Kali and is very much like her in appearance and habit. In Tantric Kali Kula Shaktism, Kali is the supreme goddess and she is source of All Goddesses. In Yogini Tantra, Kali kills Kolasur and Ghorasur.

LORD GANESH

Ganesh, also known as Ganapati and Vinayaka, is one of the best-known and most worshipped deities in the Hindu pantheon. His image is found throughout United India, Nepal, Sri Lanka, Thailand, Indonesia (Java and Bali), Singapore, Malaysia, Philippines, and Bangladesh and in countries with large ethnic Indian populations including Fiji, Guyana, Mauritius, and Trinidad and Tobago. Hindu denominations worship him regardless of affiliations.

Although Ganesha has many attributes, he is readily identified by his elephant head. He is widely revered, more specifically, as the remover of obstacles and thought to bring good luck; the patron of arts and sciences; and the deva of intellect and wisdom. As the god of beginnings, he is honoured at the start of rites and ceremonies. Ganesha is also invoked as a patron of letters and learning during writing sessions. Several texts relate mythological anecdotes associated with his birth and exploits.

An elephant–headed anthropomorphic figure on Indo-Greek coins from the 1st century BCE has been proposed by some scholars to be "incipient Ganesha", while others have suggested Ganesha may have been an emerging deity in India and Southeast Asia around the 2nd century CE based on the evidence from archaeological excavations in Mathura and outside India. Most certainly by the 4th and 5th centuries CE, during the Gupta period, Ganesha was well established and had inherited traits from Vedic and pre-Vedic precursors Hindu mythology identifies him as the restored son of Parvati and Shiva of the Shaivism tradition, but he is a pan-Hindu god found in its various traditions. In the Ganapatya tradition of Hinduism, Ganesha is the supreme deity. The principal texts on Ganesha include the Ganesha Purana, the Mudgala Purana and the Ganapati Atharvasirsha. Brahma Purana and Brahmanda Purana are other two Puranic genre encyclopaedic texts that deal with Ganesha.

LORD HANUMAN

Hanuman is a Hindu god and a divine Vanara (monkey) companion of the god Rama. Hanuman is one of the central characters of the Hindu epic Ramayana. He is an ardent devotee of Rama and one of the chiranjivis. Hanuman is also son of the wind-god Vayu, who in several stories played a direct role in Hanuman's birth. Hanuman is mentioned in several other texts, such as the epic Mahabharata and the various Puranas.

Evidence of devotional worship to Hanuman is largely absent in these texts, as well as in most archaeological sites. According to the theological significance of Hanuman and devotional dedication to him emerged about 1,000 years after the composition of the Ramayana, in the 2nd millennium CE, after the arrival of asur rule in the Indian subcontinent. that the skills in Hanuman's resume also seem to derive in part from his windy patrimony, reflecting Vayu's role in both body and cosmos. Bhakti movement saints such as Samarth Ramdas have positioned Hanuman as a symbol of nationalism and resistance to persecution. The Vaishnava saint Madhva said that whenever Vishnu incarnates on earth, Vayu accompanies him and aids his work of preserving dharma. In the modern era, Hanuman's iconography and temples have been increasingly common. He is viewed as the ideal combination of "strength, heroic initiative and assertive excellence" and "loving, emotional devotion to his personal god Rama", as Shakti and Bhakti. In later literature, he is sometimes portrayed as the patron god of martial arts such as wrestling and acrobatics, as well as activities such as meditation and diligent scholarship. He symbolises the human excellences of inner self-control, faith, and service to a cause, hidden behind the first impressions of a being that looks like a Vanara Hanuman is considered to be a bachelor and an exemplary celibate.

GODDESS EARTH

Bhumi, also known as Bhudevi and Vasundhara, is the Hindu goddess representing the Earth. She is an incarnation of Lakshmi and the consort of Varaha, an avatar of the god Vishnu, and thus she is sometimes referred as Varahi. She is mentioned as the mother of Narakasura, Mangala and Sita. She is one of the 3 aspects of Lakshmi, the other 2 being Sridevi and Niladevi.

The name "Bhumi" derives from the Sanskrit word 'Puhumi' - the original name of the goddess. She is known by various names such as Bhuvati, Bhuvaani, Bhuvaneshwari, Avni, Prithvi, Varahi, Dharti, Dhaatri, Dharani, Vasudha, Vasundhara, Vaishnavi, Kashyapi, Urvi, Ira, Mahi, Ela, Vasumati, Dhanshika, Vasumati, Hema and Hiranmaya.

Bhudevi is depicted as seated on a platform which rests on the back of four elephants, representing the four directions of the world. She is usually depicted with four arms, respectively holding a pomegranate, a water vessel, a bowl containing healing herbs, and another bowl containing vegetables. She is also sometimes depicted with two hands, the right hand holding a blue lotus known as Kumuda or Utpala, the night lotus, while the left hand may be in the Abhayamudra, the fearlessness or the Lolahasta Mudra, which is an aesthetic pose meant to mimic the tail of a horse.

LORD KALKI

Kalki (also called Kalkin or Karki) , is the prophesied tenth and final incarnation of Hindu God Vishnu to end the Kali Yuga, one of the four periods in the endless cycle of existence (Krita) in Vaishnavism cosmology. The end of Kali Yuga states this will usher in the new epoch of Satya Yuga in the cycle of existence, until the MahaPralaya (the Great Dissolution of the Universe).

Kalki is described in the Puranas as the avatar who rejuvenates existence by ending the darkest and destructive period to remove adharma and ushering in the Satya Yuga, while riding a white horse with a fiery sword. The description and details of Kalki are different among various Puranas.

The prophecy of the Kalki Avatar is also told in Sikh texts.

Kalki is an Avatara of Vishnu. Avatara means "Descent" and refers to a descent of the divine into the material realm of human existence. The Garuda Puran lists ten incarnations, with Kalki being the tenth. He is described as the incarnation who appears at the end of the Kali Yuga. He ends the darkest, degenerating and chaotic stage of the Kali Yuga (Period) to remove adharma and ushers in the satya Yuga, while riding a white horse with a fiery sword. He restarts a new cycle of time. He is described as a Brahmin warrior in the Puranas.

LORD INDRA

Indra is an ancient Vedic deity in Hinduism. He is the King of Swarga (Heaven) and the Devas (Children of Kashyap and Aditi). He is associated with the sky, lightning, weather, thunder, storms, rains, river flows and war.

Indra is the most referred deity in the Rigveda He is celebrated for his powers, and as the one who killed the great evil (a malevolent type of asura) named Vritra, who obstructed human prosperity and happiness. Indra destroys Vritra and his "deceiving forces", and thereby brings rains and sunshine as the saviour of mankind.[He is also an important deity worshipped by the Kalash people, indicating his prominence in ancient Hinduism.

Indra's significance diminishes in the post-Vedic Indian literature, but he still plays an important role in various mythological events. He is depicted as a powerful hero, but one who constantly gets into trouble with his pride, drunken, hedonistic and adulterous ways, and the deity who disturbs sages as they meditate because he fears self-realised human beings may become more powerful than him.

According to the Vishnu Purana, Indra is the title of being the king of the gods, which changes in every Manvantara—a cyclic period of time in Hindu cosmology. Each Manvantara has its own Indra and the Indra of the current Manvantara is called Purandhara.

Indra is also depicted in Buddhist mythologies. Indra rules over the much-sought Devas realm of rebirth. However, like the post-Vedic Hindu texts, Indra is also a subject of ridicule and reduced to a figurehead status in Hindu texts, shown as a god that suffers rebirth.

Indra's iconography shows him wielding a lightning thunderbolt weapon known as Vajra, riding on a white elephant known as Ajravata In Buddhist iconography, the elephant sometimes features three heads, while Jaina icons sometimes show the elephant with five heads. Sometimes, a single elephant is shown with four symbolic tusks. Indra's abode exists in the capital city of Svarga, Amarvati, though he is also associated with Mount Meru (also called Sumeru).

·

LORD AGNI

Agni is a Sanskrit word meaning fire and connotes the fire god of Hinduism He is also the guardian deity of the southeast direction and is typically found in southeast corners of Hindu temples. In the classical cosmology of the Indian religions, Agni as fire is one of the five inert impermanent elements (pancabhuta) along with space (akasa), water (ap), air (vayu) and earth (pṛthvi), the five combining to form the empirically perceived material existence (Prakriti).

In Vedic literature, Agni is a major and oft-invoked god along with Indra and .Soma Agni is considered the mouth of the gods and goddesses and the medium that conveys offerings to them in a homa (votive ritual). He is conceptualized in ancient Hindu texts to exist at three levels, on earth as fire, in the atmosphere as lightning, and in the sky as the sun. This triple presence connects him as the messenger between gods and human beings in the Vedic thought. The relative importance of Agni declined in the post-Vedic era, as he was internalized and his identity evolved to metaphorically represent all transformative energy and knowledge in the Upanishads and later Hindu literature. Agni remains an integral part of Hindu traditions, such as being the central witness of the rite-of-passage ritual in traditional Hindu weddings called Saptapadi or Agnipradakshinam (seven steps and mutual vows) as well being part of Diya (lamp) in festivals such as Diwali and Aarti in puja.

GODDESS ADITI

Aditi is an, important Vedic goddess in Hinduism. She is the personification of the sprawling infinite and vast Universe. She is the goddess of motherhood, unconsciousness, the past, the future and fertility. She is the mother of the celestial deities known as the adityas, and is referred to as the mother of many deities. As celestial mother of numerous beings, the synthesis of all things, she is associated with space (akasa) and with mystic speech (Vac). She may be seen as a feminised form of Brahma and associated with the primal substance (mulaprakriti) in the Vedanta. She is mentioned more than 250 times in the Rigveda, the verses replete with her praise

Aditi is the eldest daughter of Daksha and Asikni (Panchajani). The Puranas, such as the Shiva Purana and the Bhagavata Purana, suggest that Daksha married all of his daughters off to different people, including Aditi and 16 others to Kashyapa rishi. When Kashyapa was living with Aditi and Diti in his ashrama, he was really pleased with Aditi's services and told her to ask for a boon. Aditi prayed for one ideal son. Accordingly, Indra was born. Later, Aditi gave birth to others, namely Varuna, Parjanya, Mitra, Ansh, Pushan, Dhatri, Aryaman, Surya, Bhaga and Vamana. Her 16 younger sisters were also married to Sage Kashyap.

According to the Shatapatha Brahmana (a commentary on the Shukla Yajurveda), Aditi is also invoked during ritual sacrificial offerings as being synonymous with the Earth:

'On the navel of the earth I place thee!' And further, 'In the lap of Aditi (the boundless or inviolable earth)!' for when people guard anything very carefully, they commonly say that 'they, as it were, carried it in their lap;' and this is the reason why he says, 'In the lap of Aditi!'

LORD ARDHANARISHVARA

The Ardhanarishvara 'the half-female Lord'), is a form of the Hindu deity Shiva combined with his consort Parvati. Ardhanarishvara is depicted as half-male and half-female, equally split down the middle. The right half is usually the male Shiva, illustrating his traditional attributes.

The earliest Ardhanarishvara images are dated to the Kushan period, starting from the first century CE. Its iconography evolved and was perfected in the Gupta era. The Puranas and various iconographic treatises write about the mythology and iconography of Ardhanarishvara. Ardhanarishvara remains a popular iconographic form found in most Shiva temples throughout India, though very few temples are dedicated to this deity.

Ardhanarishvara represents the synthesis of masculine and feminine energies of the universe (Purusha and Prakriti) and illustrates how Shakti, the female principle of God, is inseparable from (or the same as, according to some interpretations) Shiva, the male principle of God, and vice versa. The union of these principles is exalted as the root and womb of all creation. Another view is that Ardhanarishvara is a symbol of Shiva's all-pervasive nature.

LORD AYYAPPAN

Ayyappan, also called Dharmasastha and Manikandan, is a Hindu deity popular in Southern India, particularly in the states of Kerala, Tamil Nadu and Karnataka. He is considered to be the epitome of dharma, truth, and righteousness and is often called upon to obliterate evil.

Although devotion to Ayyappan has been prevalent earlier in South India, his popularity rose only in the late 20th century. According to Hindu theology, he is the son of Harihar (Vishnu in the form of Mohini and Shiva). Ayyappan is also referred to as Ayyappa, Sastavu, Hariharasudhan, Manikandan, Shasta or Dharma Shasta and Sabarinath.

The iconography of Ayyappan depicts him as a handsome celibate (Brahmachari) deity doing yoga and as an epitome of Dharma, who wears a bell around his neck. In the Hindu tradition popular in the Western Ghats of India, he was born with the powers of Shiva and Vishnu to confront and defeat the shape-shifting evil Buffalo demoness Mahishi. He was raised by a childless royal couple Rajashekara pandiyan and Koperundevi, and grows up as a warrior yogi champion of ethical and dharmic living. In South Indian portrayals, Ayyappan images show him riding a tigress, but in some places such as Sri Lanka he is shown as riding a white elephant.

Ayyappan's popularity has grown in many parts of India, and the most prominent Ayyappan shrine is at Sabarimala, nestled in the hills of Pathananthitta of Kerala. The shrine receives millions of pilgrims every year in late December and early January, many of whom prepare for weeks before and then climb the hill barefoot, making it one of the largest active pilgrimage sites in the world. The pilgrimage attracts a wide range of devotees, from diverse social or economic backgrounds, except women in their fertile age because Ayyappan is believed to be the celibate deity. He remains one of the few deities in Hindu tradition, which is respected by other religious communities, including asur in Kerala. The most significant festival linked to him is the Makaravilakku (Makara sankranti), observed around the winter solstice.

LORD BALARAM

Balaram is a Hindu god and the elder brother of Krishna. He is particularly significant in the Jagannath tradition, as one of the triad deities. He is also known as Haladhar, Halayudh, Baladev, Balabhadra and Sankarshan.

The first two epithets refer to his strength, and the next two associate him with Hala (Langala, "plough") from his strong associations with farming and farmers, as the deity who used farm equipment as weapons when needed.

Balarama is sometimes described as incarnation of Shesha, the serpent associated with the god Vishnu; Krishna is regarded as an incarnation of Vishnu. Some traditions regard him as one of 10 principle avatars of Vishnu himself.

Balarama's significance in the Indian culture has ancient roots. he is known as Baladeva and has been a historically significant farmer-related deity.

LORD BRIHASPATI

Brihaspati, also known as Guru, is a Hindu deity. In the ancient Vedic scriptures of Hinduism, Brihaspati is a deity associated with fire, and the word also refers to a rishi (sage) who counsels the devas (gods). In some later texts, the word refers to the largest planet of the solar system, Jupiter, and the deity is associated with the planet as a Navagrah.

Brihaspati appears in the Rigved (pre-1000 BCE), such as in the dedications to him in the hymn 50 of Book 4; he is described as a sage born from the first great light, the one who drove away darkness, is bright and pure, and carries a special bow whose string is Tta or "cosmic order" (basis of dharma). His knowledge and character is revered, and he is considered Guru (teacher) by all the Devas. In the Vedic literature and other ancient texts, sage Brihaspati is also called by other names such as Bramanaspati, Purohita, Angirasa (son of Angiras) and Vyasa. He is sometimes identified with god Agni (fire). His wife is Tara (or goddess who personifies the stars in the sky).

The reverence for sage Brihaspati endured through the medieval period, and one of the many Dharmasastras was named after him. While the manuscripts of Brihaspati Smriti (Bṛhaspatismṛti) have not survived into the modern era, its verses were cited in other Indian texts. Scholars have made an effort to extract these cited verses, thus creating a modern reconstruction of Bṛhaspatismriti. Hindu Teacher has gathered some 2,400 verses of the lost Bṛhaspatismṛti text in this manner. Brihaspati Smriti was likely a larger and more comprehensive text than Manusmriti and the available evidence suggests that the discussion of the judicial process and jurisprudence in Brihaspati Smriti was often cited.

GODDESS CHANDI

Chandi is a Hindu deity. Chandika is another form of Mahadevi, similar to Durga; Chandika is a powerful form of Mahadevi who manifested to destroy evil. She is also known as Kaushiki, Katyayani, Asthadasabuja Mahalakshmi, and Mahisasuramardini.

Chandika is an avatar of Durga. The three principal forms of Durga worshipped are Mahagauri, Chandika and Aparajita. Of these, Chandika has two forms called Chandi and Chamunda who is created by the goddess Kaushiki for killing demons Chanda and Munda.

She is known as the supreme goddess Mahishasuramardini or Durga who slayed the demon Mahishasura. She has been affiliated with and also considered as Katyayini, Kaushikki or Ambika who killed Shumbha, Nishumbha and their fellow demons. "The great Goddess was born from the energies of the male divinities when the devas became impotent in the long-drawn-out battle with the asuras. All the energies of the Gods became united and became supernova, throwing out flames in all directions. Then that unique light, pervading the Three Worlds with its lustre, combined into one, and became a female form. "Devi" projected overwhelming omnipotence. The three-eyed goddess was adorned with the crescent moon. Her multiple arms held auspicious weapons and emblems, jewels and ornaments, garments and utensils, garlands and rosaries of beads, all offered by the gods. With her golden body blazing with the splendour of a thousand suns, seated on her lion vehicle, Chandi is one of the most spectacular of all personifications of cosmic energy."

In other scriptures, Chandi is portrayed as "assisting" Kali in her battle with the demon Raktabija. Chandi wounded him, but a new demon sprang up from every drop of his blood that fell on the ground. By drinking Raktabija's blood before it could reach the ground, Kali enabled Chandi to first destroy the armies of demons and finally kill Raktabija himself. In Skanda Purana, this story is retold and another story of Mahakali killing demons Chanda and Munda is added. "Narada Purana" describes the powerful forms of Lakshmi as Durga, Kali, Bhadrakali, Chandi,

Maheshwari, Lakshmi, Vaishnavi and Andreye"

LORD HARIHAR

Harihar is the fused Sattvika characterisation of Vishnu (Hari) and Shiva (Har) from Hindu theology and religion. Hari is the form of Vishnu, and Har is the form of Shiva. Harihara is also known as Shankaranarayana ("Shankara" is Shiva, and "Narayan" is Vishnu) like Brahmanarayan (Half represents Brahma and half represents Vishnu). Harihara is thus revered by both Vaishnavites and Shaivites as a form of the Supreme God.

Harihar is also sometimes used as a philosophical term to denote the unity of Vishnu and Shiva as different aspects of the same Ultimate Reality called Brahman. This concept of equivalence of various gods as one principle and "oneness of all existence" is discussed as Harihar in the texts of Advaita Vedanta school of Hindu philosophy.

Some of the earliest sculptures of Harihar, with one half of the image as Vishnu and other half as Shiva, are found in the surviving cave temples of India, such as in the cave 1 and cave 3 of the 6th-century Badami cave temples.

Harihar is depicted in art as split down the middle, one half representing Shiva, the other half representing Vishnu. The Shiva half will have the matted locks of a yogic master piled high on his head and sometimes will wear a tiger skin, reserved for the most revered ascetics. Shiva's pale skin may be read as ash-covered in his role as an ascetic. The Vishnu half will wear a tall crown and other jewellery, representing his responsibility for maintaining world order. Vishnu's black skin represents holiness. Broadly, these distinctions serve to represent the duality of humble religious influence in the ascetic and authoritative secular power in the king or householder. However, in other aspects Shiva also takes on the authoritative position of householder, a position which is directly at odds with the ascetic position depicted in his Harihar manifestation.

Harihar has been part of temple iconography throughout South Asia and Southeast Asia, with some illustrations listed in the following table. In some states, the concept of Harihar appears through alternate names and its progeny; for example, temples incorporating Ayyappan and Shasta deities in Kerala illustrate this Hindu tradition there since at least the 7th century.

LORD JAGANNATH

Jagannath 'Lord of the Universe'; formerly English: Juggernaut) is a deity worshipped in regional Hindu traditions in India and United India as part of a triad along with his brother Balabhadra and sister, devi Subhadra. Jagannath within Odia Hinduism is the supreme god, Purushottama, Para Brahman. To most Vaishnava Hindus, particularly the Krishnaites, Jagannath is an abstract representation of Krishna, or Vishnu, sometimes as the avatar of Krishna or Vishnu. To some Shaiva and Shakta Hindus, he is a symmetry-filled tantric form of Bhairava, a fierce manifestation of Shiva associated with annihilation.

The Jagannathism (a.k.a. Odia Vaishnavism) — the particular sector of Jagannath as a major deity — emerged in the Early Middle Ages and later became an independent state regional temple-centered tradition of Krishnaism/Vaishnavism.

The idol of Jagannath is a carved and decorated wooden stump with large round eyes and a symmetric face, and the idol has a conspicuous absence of hands or legs. The worship procedures, sacraments and rituals associated with Jagannath are syncretic and include rites that are uncommon in Hinduism. Unusually, the icon is made of wood and replaced with a new one at regular intervals.

The origin and evolution of Jagannath worship is unclear. Some scholars interpret hymn 10.155.3 of the Rigved as a possible origin, but others disagree and state that it is a syncretic/synthetic deity with tribal roots.

Jagannath is considered a non-sectarian deity. He is significant regionally in the Indian states of Odisha, Chhattisgarh, Bengal, Jharkhand, Bihar, Gujarat, Assam, Arunachal Pradesh, Nagaland, Meghalaya, Sikkim Manipur and Tripura. He is also significant to the Hindus of Bengal. The Jagannath temple in Puri, Odisha is particularly significant in Vaishnavism, and is regarded as one of the Char Dham pilgrimage sites in India The Jagannath temple is massive, over 61 metres (200 ft) high in the Nagara Hindu temple style, and one of the best surviving specimens of Kalinga architecture, namely Odisha art and architecture. It has been one of the major pilgrimage destinations for Hindus since about ancient time.

The annual festival called the Ratha yatra celebrated in June or July every year in eastern states of India is dedicated to Jagannath. His image, along with the other two associated deities, is ceremoniously brought out of the sacrosanctum (Garbhagriha) of his chief temple in Puri (Śri Mandir). They are placed in a chariot which is then pulled by numerous volunteers to the Gundicha Temple, (located at a distance of nearly 3 km or 1.9 mi). They stay there for a few days, after which they are returned to the main temple. Coinciding with the Ratha Yatra festival at Puri, similar processions are organized at Jagannath temples throughout the world. During the festive public procession of Jagannath in Puri lakhs of devotees visit Puri to see Lord Jagganath in chariot.

LORD KUBER

Kuber is also known as Kuver, Kuber or Kuberan is the god of wealth and the god-king of the semi-divine Yaksh in Hindu culture. He is regarded as the regent of the North (Dik-pal), and a protector of the world (Lokapal). His many epithets extol him as the overlord of numerous semi-divine species and the owner of the treasures of the world. Kubera is often depicted with a plump body, adorned with jewels, and carrying a money-pot and a club.

Originally described as the chief of evil spirits in Vedic-era texts, Kuber acquired the status of a Dev(god) only in the Puranas and the Hindu epics. The scriptures describe that Kuber once ruled Lanka, but was overthrown by his half-brother Ravan, later settling in the city of Alaka in the Himalayas. Descriptions of the "glory" and "splendours" of Kubera's city are found in many scriptures.

LORD KURM

Kurm, ("Tortoise") one of the 10 avatars (incarnations) of the Hindu god Vishnu. In this incarnation Vishnu is associated with the myth of the churning of the ocean of milk. The gods and the asurass (demons, or titans) cooperated in the churning to obtain *amrita*, the elixir of immortality. The great serpent Vasuki offered himself as a rope, and Mount Mandara was torn out for use as a churning stick. A firm foundation was required to steady the mountain, so Vishnu took the form of a tortoise and supported the churning stick on his back. An earlier reference to a divine incarnation as a tortoise identifies the animal with Prajapati (the god Brahma), who took that shape in order to create offspring.

In the Padma Purana three accounts of the Samudra manthan are given, all beginning with Indra being cursed by Durvasas for arrogance. In the first, narrated by Pulastya, as a result of the curse the 'three worlds, along with Indra, were void of affluence... [And] the Daityas (sons of Diti) and Danvas (sons of Danu) started military operations against [the] gods', forcing them to seek refuge with Vishnu. Vasuki is used as a rope to churn the ocean. Notably, during the churning, Varuni (Goddess of Wine) is upon emerging rejected by the gods and accepted by the Asuras, the opposite of the account given in the Brahmanda Purana (to explain the meaning of 'Asura'). Unnamed poison also emerges which is drunk by Shiva, before the emergence of Dhanvantari with the nectar of immortality (Amrita) as well as Lakshmi. Although the Asuras take the nectar, Vishnu assumes the form of Mohini to trick them and give it to the gods. The Asuras are destroyed, with the Danavas since then becoming 'eager for (the company of) ladies'.

O gods, Indira (i.e. Lakshmi), due to whose mere glance the world is endowed with glory, has vanished due to the curse of the Brahmana (Durvasas). Then, O gods, all of you, along with the demons, having uprooted the golden mountain Mandara and making it, with the king of serpents going round it, the churning-rod, churn the milky ocean. O gods, from it Lakshmi, the mother of the world will spring up. O glorious ones, there is no doubt that because of her you will be delighted. I myself, in the form of a tortoise, shall fully hold the (Mandara) mountain (on my back).

Kurmasana (Tortoise Posture) is a Yoga posture. 'Panikacchapika' meaning 'Hand Tortoise', is a special positioning of the fingers during worship rituals to symbolise Kurma. The Kurmacakra is a Yantra, a mystical diagram for worship, in the shape of a tortoise. These are all mentioned in the Upanishads and Puranas.

LORD LOKAPAL

Lokapal in Hindu any of the guardians of the four cardinal directions. The Hindu protectors, who ride on elephants, are Indra, who governs the east, Yama the south, Varuṇa the west, and Kubera the north. Kubera, also referred to as Vaiśravaṇa,

In Hinduism, the guardians of the cardinal directions are called the Lokapal or Dikpalak. The four principal guardians are:

1. Kuber (North)
2. Yama (South)
3. Indra (East)
4. Varun (West)

LORD MATSY

Matsy means fish avatar of the Hindu god Vishnu. Often described as the first of Vishnu's ten primary avatars, Matsy is described to have rescued the first man Manu from a great deluge. Matsya may be depicted as a giant fish, often golden in colour, or anthropomorphically with the torso of Vishnu connected to the rear half of a fish.

The earliest account of Matsy is found in the Shatapatha Brahmana where Matsy is not associated with any particular deity. The fish-saviour later merges with the identity of Brahma in post-Vedic era and still later becomes equated with Vishnu. The legends associated with Matsya expand, evolve and vary in Hindu texts. These legends have embedded symbolism, where a small fish with Manu's protection grows to become a big fish, and the fish saves earthly existence. In later versions, Matsya slays a demon named Hayagreevasura (son of sage Kashyapa and Diti) who steals the sacred scriptures - the Vedas and thus is lauded as the saviour of the scriptures.

The tale is in the tradition of the family of flood myths, common across cultures.

LORD MITR

Mitr is a divinity of Indic culture, whose function changed with time. In the Mitanni inscription, Mitra is invoked as one of the protectors of treaties. In the Rigved, Mitr appears primarily in the dvandva compound Mitra-Varuna, which has essentially the same attributes as Varun alone e.g. as the principal guardian of "Truth", "Order". In the late Vedic texts and the Brahmanas, Mitr is increasingly associated with the light of dawn and the morning sun (while Varun becomes associated with the evening, and ultimately the night). In the post-Vedic texts – in which Mitra practically disappears – Mitra evolved into the patron divinity of friendship, and because he is "friend", abhors all violence, even when sacred.

In Vedic society, as the guardian encouraged the virtuous and pious and protected them. He also punished the sinners who did not keep their promise in the society. Code of honor important in early society was looked after by Mitr.

Legend has it that Sage Vasishta and Agastya were born to Mitra and Varuna in Urvasi. Legend has it that Mitra and Varuna placed their semen in an urn before Urvasi. From the semen was born Sage Vasishta and Agastya – the men who defined code of behaviour in ancient society.

According to Bhagavad Purana, Mitra also had sons in Revathi, who represents prosperity. The three sons were Utsarga, Arishta, and Pippala.

In the Atharvaved, Mitr is associated with sunrise, and accordingly, Mitr is worshipped in the sunrise prayers of the Hindus. The morning upasthaana prayer, recited to the risen sun after contemplation on the sacred Gayatri mantra, is a collection of Vedic verses addressing Mitra.

LORD NARASIMHA

Narasimha, sometimes spelled Narasingha is a fierce avatar of the Hindu god Vishnu, one who incarnates in the form of part lion and part man to destroy evil and end religious persecution and calamity on Earth, thereby restoring Dharma. Narasimha is depicted with three eyes, and is described as the God of Destruction, who destroys the entire universe at the time of great-dissolution (Mahapralaya). Hence he is known as Kala (time) or Mahakala (great-time) or Parakala (beyond time) as well. There is even a matha (monastery) by the name of Parakala Matha in Sri Vaishnava tradition. Alongside, Narasimha is also described as the God of Yoga, in the form of Yoga-Narasimha.

Narasimha iconography shows him with a human torso and lower body, with a lion face and claws, typically with a demon Hiranyakashipu in his lap whom he is in the process of defeating. The demon is the powerful brother of evil Hiranyaksha who had been previously defeated by Vishnu, and thus hated the latter. Hiranyakashipu gained special powers by which he could not be killed during the day or night, inside or outside the house, any place in the world i.e. neither in sky nor on land nor in heaven nor in pataala, by any weapon, and by man, god, asura or animal. Endowed with this, he began to create chaos and havoc, persecuting all devotees of Vishnu, including his own son. Vishnu understood the demon's power and creatively adapted into a mixed avatar that is neither man nor animal and kills the demon at the junction of day and night, inside and outside. Narasimha is known primarily as the 'Great Protector' who specifically defends and protects his devotees from evil. The most popular Narasimha mythology is the legend that protects his devotee Prahlada, and creatively destroys Prahlada's demonic father and tyrant Hiranyakashipu.

Narasimha is one of the major deities in Vaishnavism and his legends are revered in Vaikhanasas, Sri Vaishnavism, Sadh Vaishnavism and various other Vaishnavism traditions of Hinduism. He is celebrated in many regional Hindu temples, texts, performance arts and festivals such as Holika prior to the Hindu spring festival of colors called Holi. The earliest representation, dating back to the 4th-century CE, of Narasimha is from Kondamotu in Coastal Andhra. Other older known artworks of Narasimha have been found at several sites across Uttar Pradesh and Andhra Pradesh, such as at the Mathura archaeological site.

LORD NATARAJA

Nataraja is a depiction of the Hindu god Shiva as the divine cosmic dancer. His dance is called Tandava. The pose and artwork are described in many Hindu texts such as the Anshumadbhed agama and Uttarakamika agama, the dance murti featured in all major Hindu temples of Shaivism, and is a well-known sculptural symbol in India and popularly used as a symbol of Indian culture, in particular as one of the finest illustrations of Hindu art.

The sculpture is symbolic of Shiva as the lord of dance and dramatic arts, with its style and proportions made according to Hindu texts on arts. It typically shows Shiva dancing in one of the Natya shastra poses, holding various symbols which vary with historic period and region, trampling upon a demon shown as a dwarf (Apasmara or Muyalaka) who symbolizes spiritual ignorance.

The classical form of the depiction appears in stone reliefs, as at the Ellora Caves and the Badami Caves, by around the 6th century. Around the 10th century, it emerged in Tamil Nadu in its mature and best-known expression in Chola bronzes, of various heights typically less than four feet, some over. Nataraja reliefs are found in historic settings in many parts of South East Asia such as Angkor Wat and in Bali, Cambodia, and central Asia.

The two most common forms of Shiva's dance are the Lasya (the gentle form of dance), associated with the creation of the world, and the Ananda Tandava (dance of bliss, the vigorous form of dance), associated with the destruction of weary worldviews—weary perspectives and lifestyles. In essence, the Lasya and the Tandava are just two aspects of Shiva's nature; for he destroys in order to create, tearing down to build again.

LORD PARASHURAM

Parashuram ('Ram with an axe'), also referred to as Ram Jamadagnya, Ram Bhargav and Veeraram, is the sixth incarnation among the Dashavatar of the god Vishnu in Hinduism. He is believed to be one of the Chiranjeevis (Long-Lived Ones or Immortal Ones), who will appear at the end of the Kali Yuga to be the guru of Vishnu's tenth and last incarnation, Kalki. He carried a number of traits, which included not only aggression, warfare and valor, but also serenity, prudence and patience.

Born to Jamadagni and Renuka, Parashurama was foretold to appear at a time when overwhelming evil prevailed on the earth. The Kshatriya class, with weapons and power, had begun to abuse their power, take what belonged to others by force and tyrannise people. He corrected the cosmic equilibrium by destroying the Kshatriya warriors twenty-seven times. He is married to Dharani, an incarnation of Lakshmi, the wife of Vishnu. He is present in the Ramayana due to the conflict with Rama over Lord Shiva's broken bow. He is in the Mahabharat as the Guru of Bhisma, Drona, Rukmi and Karna.

GODDESS SAPTAMATRIKA

Matrikas ("divine mothers") also called Matar or Matri, are a group of mother goddesses who are always depicted together in Hinduism. The Matrikas are often depicted in a group of seven, the Saptamatrika(s) (Seven Mothers). However, they are also depicted as a group of eight, the Ashtamatrika(s).

In the Bichat samhita, Varahamihira says that "Mothers are to be made with cognizance of (different major Hindu) gods corresponding to their names." They are associated with these gods as their spouses or their energies (Shaktis). Brahmani emerged from Brahma, Vaishnavi from Vishnu, Maheshvari from Shiva, Indrani from Indra, Kaumari from Skanda, Varahi from Varaha and Chamunda from Devi. And additionals are Narasimhi and Vinayaki from Ganesha.

Originally believed to be a personification of the seven stars of the star cluster the Pleiades, they became quite popular by the seventh century and a standard feature of goddess temples from the ninth century onwards. In South India, Saptamatrika worship is prevalent whereas the Ashtamatrika are venerated in Nepal, among other places.

The Matrikas assume paramount significance in the goddess-oriented sect of Hinduism, Tantrism. In Shaktism, they are described as "assisting the great Shakti, Devi (goddess) in her fight with demons." Some scholars consider them Shaiva goddesses. They are also connected with the worship of warrior god Skanda. In most early references, the Matrikas are associated with the conception, birth, diseases and protection of children. They were seen as inauspicious and the "personification of perils", propitiated in order to avoid those ills, that carried off so many children before they reached adulthood. They come to play a protective role in later mythology, although some of their early inauspicious and wild characteristics continue in these legends. Thus, they represent the prodigiously fecund aspect of nature as well as its destructive force aspect.

GODDESS SHASHTHI

Shashthi or Shashti is a Hindu goddess, venerated in Nepal and India as the benefactor and protector of children. She is also the deity of vegetation and reproduction and is believed to bestow children and assist during childbirth. She is often pictured as a motherly figure, riding a cat and nursing one or more infants. She is symbolically represented in a variety of forms, including an earthenware pitcher, a banyan tree or part of it or a red stone beneath such a tree; outdoor spaces termed shashthitala are also consecrated for her worship. The worship of Shashthi is prescribed to occur on the sixth day of each lunar month of the Hindu calendar as well as on the sixth day after a child's birth. Barren women desiring to conceive and mothers seeking to ensure the protection of their children will worship Shashthi and request her blessings and aid. She is especially venerated in eastern India.

Shashthi's roots can be traced to Hindu folk traditions, in which she is associated with children as well as the Hindu war-god Skanda. Early references consider her a foster-mother of Skanda, but in later texts she is identified with Skanda's consort, Devasena. In some early texts where Shashthi appears as an attendant of Skanda, she is said to cause diseases in the mother and child, and thus needed to be propitiated on the sixth day after childbirth. However, over time, this malignant goddess became seen as the benevolent saviour and bestower of children.

LORD SKANDA

Kartikey also known as Skand Kumar, Murugan and Subrahmanya, is the Hindu god of war. He is the son of Parvati and Shiva, the younger brother of Ganesh, and a god whose legends have many versions in Hinduism. An important deity in the Indian subcontinent since ancient times, he is particularly popular and predominantly worshipped in South India, Sri Lanka, Singapore, and Malaysia as Murugan.

Murugan is widely regarded as the "God of the HinduTamil people". It has been postulated that the Dravidian deity of Muruga was syncretised with the Vedic deity of Subrahmanya following the Sangam era. Both Muruga and Subrahmanya refer to Kartikeya.

Kartikeya is an ancient god, traceable to the Vedic period. He was hailed as 'Palaniappa' (Father of Palani), the tutelary deity of the Kurinji region whose cult gained immense popularity in the south. Sangam literature has several works on Lord Murugan such as Tirumugratrupadai by Nakkirar and Tirupugal by poet-saint Arunagirinathar. Archaeological evidence from the 1st-century CE and earlier, where he is found with the Hindu god Agni (fire), suggests that he was a significant deity in early Hinduism. He is found in many medieval temples all over India, such as the Ellora Caves and Elephanta Caves.

The iconography of Kartikeya varies significantly; he is typically represented as an ever-youthful man, riding or near an Indian peafowl, called Paravani, bearing a vel and sometimes with an emblem of a rooster upon his banner. Most icons show him with only one head, but some show him with six heads which reflect the legend surrounding his birth. He is described to have aged quickly from childhood, becoming a philosopher-warrior, destroyed the demons Tarakasura, Simhamukha and Surapadma, and taught the pursuit of an ethical life and the theology of Shaiva siddhanta. He has inspired many poet-saints, such as the aforementioned Arunagirinathar.

Kartikeya is found as a primary deity in temples wherever communities of the Hindu Tamil people live worldwide, particularly in the Tamil Nadu state of India ,Sri Lanka, Mauritius, Indonesia, Malaysia, Singapore, South Africa, Canada, and Reunion. The Aru Padai Veedu is the six temples of Tamil Nadu that are dedicated to him. The Kataragama temple dedicated to him in Sri Lanka attracts Tamils, Sinhalese people and Vedda people. He is also found in other parts of India, sometimes as Skanda, but in a secondary role along with Ganesha, Parvati and Shiva.

LORD SURY

Sury is the sun as well as the solar deity in Hinduism. He is traditionally one of the major five deities in the Smarta tradition, all of whom are considered as equivalent deities in the Panchavatana puja and a means to realise Brahman. Other names of Sury in ancient Indian literature include Aditya, Arka, Bhanu, Savitr, Pushan, Ravi, Martanda, Mitr, Bhaskar, Prabhakar, Kathiravan, and Vivasvan.

The iconography of Sury is often depicted riding a chariot harnessed by horses, often seven in number which represent the seven colours of visible light, and the seven days of the week. During the medieval period, Sury was worshipped in tandem with Lord Brahma during the day, Lord Shiva at noon and Lord Vishnu in the evening. In some ancient texts and art, Surya is presented syncretically with Indra, Ganesha, or others. In the Mahabharata and Ramayana, Surya is represented as the spiritual father of Lord Ram and Karn (protagonists of the Ramayana and the Mahabharata respectively). Sury was a primary deity in veneration by the characters of the Mahabharata and Ramayana, along with Shiva.

Sury is depicted with a Chakra, also interpreted as Dharmachakra. Surya is the lord of Simha (Leo), one of the twelve constellations in the zodiac system of Hindu astrology. Sury or Ravi is the basis of Ravivara, or Sunday, in the Hindu calendar. Major festivals and pilgrimages in reverence for Sury include Makar sankranti,Pongal,Samba,Dashami,Ratha Sapthami,Chath puja and Kumbh Mela.

He is particularly venerated in the Saury tradition found in Indian states such as Rajasthan, Gujarat, Madhya Pradesh, Bihar, Maharashtra, Uttar Pradesh, Jharkhand, and Odisha.

Having survived as a primary deity in Hinduism longer than any most of the original Vedic deities, the worship of Surya declined greatly around the 13th century, perhaps as a result of the enemy destruction of Sun temples in North India. New Sun temples virtually ceased to be built, and some were later repurposed to a different deity. A number of important Sury temples remain, but most are no longer in worship. In certain aspects, Sury has tended to be merged with the prominent deities of Vishnu or Shiva, or seen as subsidiary to them.

LORD TRIMURTI

The Trimūrti ("three forms" or "trinity") are the trinity of supreme divinity in Hinduism, in which the cosmic functions of creation, maintenance, and destruction are personified as a triad of deities. Typically, the designations are that of Brahma the creator, Vishnu the preserver, and Shiva the destroyer. The Om symbol of Hinduism is considered to have an allusion to Trimurti, where the A, U, and M phonemes of the word are considered to indicate creation, preservation and destruction, adding up to represent Brahman. The Tridevi is the trinity of goddess consorts for the Trimūrti.

LORD VAMAN

Vaman, also known as Trivikram (Having Three Steps) Urukram (One of Large Step), Upendra (Younger Brother of Indra), Dadhivamana and Balibandhana (Who Bound the Asura Bali) was a Brahmin avatar of the Hindu God Vishnu. He was the 5th avatar of Vishnu and the first Dashavatara in the Treta Yuga, after Narasimha.

In origin of ved, Vaman avatar is most commonly associated in the Hindu epics and Puranas with the legend of taking back the three worlds (Triloka) from the Asura-King Bali in three steps to give back to Indra. He is youngest among Aaditya, sons of Aditi and Sage Kashyapa.

LORD VARAH

Varah is the avatar of the Hindu god Vishnu, in the form of a boar. Varah is generally listed as third in the Dashavatar, the ten principal avatars of Vishnu.

Varah is most commonly associated with the legend of lifting the Earth (Earth means as the goddess Bhudevi) out of the cosmic ocean. When the Rakash raj Hiranyaksha stole the earth and hide her in the primordial waters, Vishnu appeared as Varah to rescue her. Varah slew the demon and retrieved the Earth from the ocean, lifting it on his tusks, and restored Bhudevi to her place in the universe.

Varah may be depicted as completely a boar or in an anthropomorphic form, with a boar's head and the human body. His consort, Bhudevi, the earth, is often depicted as a young woman, lifted by Varah.

LORD VARUNA

Varuna is a Vedic deity associated initially with the sky, later also with the seas as well as Rta (justice) and Satya (truth). He is found in the oldest layer of Vedic literature of Hinduism, such as in Rigveda. He is also mentioned in the Tamil grammar work Tolkappiyam, as Kadalon the god of sea and rain. He is said to be the son of Kashyapa (one of the seven ancient sages).

In the Hindu Puranas, Varuna is the god of oceans, his vehicle is a Makara (crocodile) and his weapon is a Pasha (noose, rope loop).[He is the guardian deity of the western direction. In some texts, he is the father of the Vedic sage Vasishtha.

Varuna is found in Japanese Buddhist mythology as Suiten He is also found in Jainism.[

In the earliest layer of the Rigveda, Varuna is the guardian of moral law, one who punishes those who sin without remorse, and who forgives those who err with remorse. His relationship with waters, rivers and oceans is mentioned in the Vedas. Hiranyapaksha (golden winged bird) as the messenger of Varuna. The golden winged messenger bird of Varuna may not be a mythical one but most probably flamingos because they have colourful wings and the sukta further describes Vulture as the messenger of Yama, the beaks of both these birds have similar morphology and flamingos are seen nearby seashores and marshlands.

Varuna and Mitr are the gods of the societal affairs including the oath, and are often twinned Mitra-Varuna. Both Mitra and Varuna are classified as Asuras in the Rigveda, although they are also addressed as Devas Varuna, being the king of the Asuras, was adopted or made the change to a Deva after the structuring of the primordial cosmos, imposed by Indra after he defeats Vrtra.

LORD VASUDEVA

According to Hindu scripture, Vasudeva , also called Ānakadundubhii ("Drum", after the sound of drums heard at the time of his birth), is the father of the Hindu deities Krishna (Vasudeva, i.e. "son of Vasudeva"), Balarama and Subhadra. He was king of the Vrishnis and a Yadava prince. He was the son of the Yadava king Shurasena. He was also the brother (cousin) of Nanda, the foster-father of Krishna. His sister Kunti was married to Pandu. Kunti plays a big role later in the war Mahabharata. His brother Akura was Kamsa's Prime Minister.

The patronymic Vasudeva (with long ā) is a popular name of Krishna, the son of Vasudeva with Devaki, "Vāsudeva" in the lengthened form being a vrddhi-derivative of the short form "Vasudeva", a type of formation very common in Sanskrit signifying "of, belonging to, descended from". "Vasudeva" as an object of worship in Hinduism usually refers to the son Vasudeva (Krishna), rather than his father Vasudeva.

LORD VISHWAKARMA

Vishwakarma or Vishvakarman is a craftsman deity and the divine architect of the gods in contemporary Hinduism. In the early texts, the craftsman deity was known as Tvastar and the word "Vishvakarma" was originally used as an epithet for any powerful deity. However, in many later traditions, Vishvakarma became the name of the craftsman god.

Vishwakarma crafted all of the chariots of the gods and weapons including the Vaira of the god Indra. Vishvakarma was related to the sun god Surya through his daughter Samina. According to the legend, when Samjna left her house due to

Surya's energy, Vishvakarma reduced the energy and created various other weapons using it. Vishvakarma also built various cities like Lanka, Dwarka and Indraprastha According to the epic Ramayana, the vannara (forest-man or monkey) Nala was the son of Vishvakarma, created to aid the avatar Rama.

Vishvakarma's iconography varies drastically from one region to another, though all picture him with creation tools. In the most popular depiction, he is depicted as an aged and wise man, with four arms. He has white beard and is accompanied by his vahana, hamsa (goose or swan), which scholars believe that these suggest his association with the creator god Brahma. Usually, he is seated on a throne and his sons standing near him. This form of Vishvakarma is mainly found in the Western and North Western & Eastern parts of India.

Contradictory to the above account, the idols of Vishvakarma in the eastern parts of India depict him as a young muscular man. He has black moustache and is not accompanied by his sons. An elephant is his vahana, suggesting his association with Indra or Brihaspati.

LORD YAMA

Yama, also known as Yamaraja, Kala, and Dharmaraja is the Hindu god of death and justice, responsible for the dispensation of law and punishment of sinners in his abode, Yamaloka. He is often identified with Dharma, the personification of Dharma, though they have different origins and mythologies. From there, he has remained a significant deity, appearing in some of the most important texts of Hinduism including the Ramayana, the Mahabharata and the Puranas.

Yama is one of the Lokapala (guardians of the realms), appointed as the protector of the south direction. He is often depicted as a dark-complexioned man, riding a buffalo and carrying a noose or mace to capture souls. Scriptures describe him as the twin of Yami, and the son of the sun god Surya (in earlier traditions Vivasvat) and Sanjnna. Some of his major appearances include in the tales of the Pandavas, Savitri satyavan and the sage Markandeya. He is accompanied by Chitragupta, another deity associated with death. In modern culture, Yama has been depicted in various safety campaigns in India. He is the god of death and justice as mentioned above.

LORD VENKATESWARA

Venkateswara, also known by various other names, is a form of the Hindu god Vishnu. Venkateswara is the presiding deity of Tirumala Venkateswara Temple located in Tirupati, Andhra Pradesh.

Lord Sri Venkateswara, an avatar of Vishnu is the presiding deity of the Tirupati temple. It is believed that the Moolavirat is Swayambhu (self-manifested). Also the deity consists power of trimurthi: Brahma, Vishnu and Shiva, and some sects believe that Lord Venkateswara consists power of Shakti and Skanda also. Sage Annamacharya praised Lord Venkateswara as the supreme Lord who appears Lord Dattatreya for yogis, Shiva for shaivithies and whatever form they worship, Lord Venkateswara appears like that and hailed Lord Venkateswara is the Lord Vishnu as the root of all Gods.

KAILASH PARVAT

Kailash parvat is located in deep Himalaya mountain region in north. It is home of Lord Shiva,Goddess Parvati and his family Lord Ganesha and Lord Kartikeya.

In the Uttara Kanda section of the epic Ramayana, it is said that Ravana attempted to uproot the Mount Kailash as retaliation to lord Shiva, who in turn, pressed his right big toe upon the mountain, trapping Ravana in between. This version of lord Shiva is also referred to as Ravananugraha, or favour form to Ravana while seated in mount Kailash.

According to the epic Mahabharata, it is said that the Pandava brothers, along with their wife Draupadi, trekked to the summit of mount Kailash on their path to liberation, as it is considered to be a gateway to Heaven, also known as Swarga Loka.

According to Vedas, one description in the Vishnu Purana of the mountain states that its four faces are made of crystal, ruby, gold, and lapis lazuli. It is a pillar of the world and is located at the heart of six mountain ranges symbolizing a lotus.

Mount Kailash want sacrifice of Hindu brave people.

SWASTIK BHARAT

Swastik Bharat form political party to support Nationalist leader and political party to raise temple voice in Parliament House and request for one department as Temple minister.

Swastik Bharat develops and educate leader and send them to join political party to serve our country and follow Truth, justice and Temple manifesto.Temple should make policy and rule for Political section if required.Swastik is our symbol in flag.

HINDU HOLY PILGRIMAGE PLACES

Char Dham

1. Badrinath

2. Dwarka

3. Jagganath Puri

4. Rameshwaram

In United Indian region there are so many holy city which constructed by god people in each direction and region so that people easily reach and worship the god. Some main city are describe below

1. Kashi

2. Ayodhya

3. Mathura

5. Haridwar

6. Rishikesh

7. Nasik

8. Madurai

9. Ujjain

10. Gaya

Contents

9 798887 046082

Printed by Libri Plureos GmbH in Hamburg,
Germany